Tadpoles
Nursery Rhymes

ʌis Little Pig

and

is Dippy Dog

Notes for adults

TADPOLES NURSERY RHYMES are structured to provide support for newly independent readers. The books may also be used by adults for sharing with young children.

The language of nursery rhymes is often already familiar to an emergent reader, so the opportunity to see these rhymes in print gives a highly supportive early reading experience. The alternative rhymes extend this reading experience further, and encourage children to play with language and try out their own rhymes.

If you are reading this book with a child, here are a few suggestions:

1. Make reading fun! Choose a time to read when you and the child are relaxed and have time to share the story.
2. Recite the nursery rhyme together before you start reading. What might the alternative rhyme be about? Why might the child like it?
3. Encourage the child to reread the rhyme, and to retell it in their own words, using the illustrations to remind them what has happened.
4. Point out together the rhyming words when the whole rhymes are repeated or pages 12 and 22 (developing phonological awareness will help with decoding language) and encourage the child to make up their own alternative rhymes.
5. Give praise! Remember that small mistakes need not always be corrected.

First published in 2008 by
Franklin Watts
338 Euston Road
London NW1 3BH

Franklin Watts Australia
Level 17/207 Kent Street
Sydney NSW 2000

Text (This Dippy Dog) © Brian Moses 2008
Illustration © Lisa Williams 2008

The rights of Brian Moses to be identified as the author of This Dippy Dog and Lisa Williams as the illustrator of this Work have been asserted in accordance with the Copyright, Designs and Patents Act, 1988.

ISBN 978 0 7496 8020 6 (hbk)
ISBN 978 0 7496 8027 5 (pbk)

Series Editor: Jackie Hamley
Series Advisor: Dr Hilary Minns
Series Designer: Peter Scoulding

Printed in China

Franklin Watts is a division of Hachette Children's Books an Hachette Livre UK company.
www.hachettelivre.co.uk

This Little
Pig

Retold by Brian Moses
Illustrated by Lisa Williams

W
FRANKLIN WATTS
LONDON•SYDNEY

Lisa Williams

"I love drawing dogs and pigs. Do you have a dog at home? Maybe you could try drawing a picture of your dog – that is if he will stay still for you!"

This little pig went
to market.

This little pig had roast beef.

This little pig had none.

And this little pig cried, "Wee-wee-wee-wee,"

This Little Pig

This little pig went to market.

This little pig stayed at home.

This little pig had roast beef.

This little pig had none.

And this little pig cried,

"Wee-wee-wee-wee,"

all the way home!

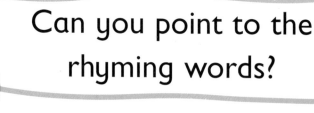

Can you point to the
rhyming words?

This Dippy
Dog

by Brian Moses
Illustrated by Lisa Williams

Brian Moses

"I have a dippy dog called Honey who likes to chase the squirrels that visit her garden. She never catches them but likes to think that one day she might!"

This dippy dog stole sausages.

This dippy dog
stole a bone.

This dippy dog
chased squirrels.

This dippy dog
chased none.

And this dippy dog went,
"Yap-yap-yap-yap,"

on his mobile phone!

Yap-yap-yap-yap-yap

This Dippy Dog

This dippy dog stole sausages.

This dippy dog stole a bone.

This dippy dog chased squirrels.

This dippy dog chased none.

And this dippy dog went,

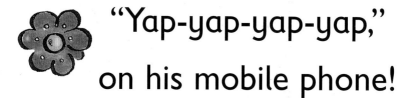

"Yap-yap-yap-yap,"

on his mobile phone!

Can you point to the
rhyming words?

Puzzle Time!

How many little pigs and dippy dogs can you count?

Answers

There are 5 little pigs and 4 dippy dogs in the picture!